Jasper John Dooley
NOT in Love

Jasper John Dooley
NOT in Love

Written by Caroline Adderson
Illustrated by Ben Clanton

Kids Can Press

For Lucy H. — C.A.

Text © 2014 Caroline Adderson
Illustrations © 2014 Ben Clanton

This is a work of fiction and any resemblance of characters to persons living or dead is purely coincidental.

Kids Can Press acknowledges the financial support of the Government of Ontario, through the Ontario Media Development Corporation's Ontario Book Initiative; the Ontario Arts Council; the Canada Council for the Arts; and the Government of Canada, through the CBF, for our publishing activity.

Published in Canada by
Kids Can Press Ltd.
25 Dockside Drive
Toronto, ON M5A 0B5

Published in the U.S. by
Kids Can Press Ltd.
2250 Military Road
Tonawanda, NY 14150

www.kidscanpress.com

Edited by Sheila Barry and Yasemin Uçar
Designed by Marie Bartholomew

This book is smyth sewn casebound.
Manufactured in Shen Zhen, Guang Dong, P.R. China, in 10/2013, by Printplus Limited

CM 14 0 9 8 7 6 5 4 3 2 1

Library and Archives Canada Cataloguing in Publication

Adderson, Caroline, 1963–, author
    Jasper John Dooley not in love / written by Caroline Adderson ;
illustrated by Ben Clanton.

(Jasper John Dooley ; 3)
ISBN 978-1-55453-803-4 (bound)

I. Clanton, Ben, 1988–, illustrator II. Title. III. Series: Adderson, Caroline, 1963– . Jasper John Dooley ; 3.

PS8551.D3267J37 2014   jC813'.54   C2013-904117-6

Kids Can Press is a *l⦿rus*™ Entertainment company

Contents

Chapter 1

Jasper John Dooley and Ori were playing knights with Leon at lunch. They ran around in the bushes at the back of the schoolyard where the playground monitor couldn't see them. Jasper and Ori waved sticks. They chased Leon, who didn't have a stick. Chasing people with sticks wasn't allowed at their school. If a real dragon showed up, they probably wouldn't be allowed to chase it with sticks either. The principal would say it was Very Dangerous.

Jasper and Ori ran after their dragon, but Leon was too fast. "Hey!" Jasper shouted. "Slow down or we'll never slay you!"

"What's slay?" Leon shouted back.

"Kill!" Ori shouted. "But when you're talking about dragons, you're supposed to say 'slay'!"

Leon stopped running. Jasper caught up and flicked his stick across Leon's stomach. Leon let out a terrible roar.

"Sorry," Jasper said.

Leon wrapped his arms around his middle. He crumpled on the ground, rolling around and roaring "Agh! Rawr! Grrr!"

Finally, he stopped. Jasper and Ori peered down. "Are you okay, Leon?"

"No," Leon said. "I'm dead."

Jasper laughed. "That's one dragon for me," he told Ori. He told Leon, "You can get up now."

Leon didn't get up. He lay there like he was really dead. Even when Jasper and Ori dropped their sticks and tickled Leon, he wouldn't stop being dead. Even when they said the playground monitor was coming over, Leon wouldn't get up. So Jasper and Ori ran off before the monitor got there and asked who slayed Leon.

They went to climb on the jungle gym for the last ten minutes of lunch. Zoë and Isabel were on the swings. As soon as they saw the boys, they wanted them to play babies. The two girls loved playing babies, but the two boys would only play if the girls had something to pay them with. Leftover Halloween candy was good, or cookies from their lunches.

"No cookies, no babies," Jasper said.

Isabel smiled, showing she had no front teeth. From her pocket she took two small, square packets of jam like you get in restaurants.

"The thing is," Ori said to Jasper, "I'd be a baby for jam."

So would Jasper.

Isabel was always Ori's mother and Zoë was always Jasper's. The babies lay down in the grass and wa-wa-waed while the mothers went to collect food. Food was pinecones and twigs. The babies only got their candy or cookie at the end, for playing properly.

While Jasper and Ori were wa-wa-waing in the grass, the playground monitor came over and said, "I don't know what's going on today. There's another boy lying on the ground over there." She pointed to the bushes at the back of the playground.

"Wa-wa-wa-wa!" the boys cried so she wouldn't ask who slayed Leon.

A few minutes later the two mothers showed up with pinecones. They got down on their knees and hauled their babies onto their laps. Jasper hated this part.

"Wa-wa-wa-wa!" he cried. "Wa-wa-wa-wa!"

Zoë pushed a pinecone in Jasper's face. He was supposed to pretend to eat it. Ori was pretending, but Jasper got an idea. "I want my jam now," he said.

"No. You'll run away," Zoë said.

"I won't. I'll run away if you *don't* give me my jam."

Zoë took a jam packet from Isabel. She said she would feed it to Jasper. She peeled off the cover and used a twig as a spoon. Jasper opened his mouth and ate a twigful of the sweet jam. Like a real baby, he grabbed the twig and smeared jam around his mouth. Then he said, "Do you see what's on my face?"

"Jam," Zoë said.

"No, it's blood," Jasper said. "I'm a bad baby!"

Ori jumped up, too, and said, "We're bad, bad babies!"

The girls screamed and ran away. And then the bell rang.

After lunch, Ms. Tosh asked everybody to get together with their reading buddies. Jasper and Ori were reading buddies. They were reading buddies, knights, friends and neighbors. Ori lived across the alley and one house down from Jasper.

Before anybody else could, Jasper and Ori dove

into the Book Nook at the back of the classroom and stretched out on the cozy pillows.

"You read first," Ori said.

Jasper grabbed a book. But instead of reading out loud to Ori, he started chewing on the book. "I'm still a bad baby," he told Ori. "And I eat books."

"Don't," Ori whispered. "Stop."

Leon, who wasn't dead anymore, turned around at his table. When he saw Jasper eating his book, he laughed and pointed so that everybody in the class turned to look.

Ms. Tosh didn't laugh. She said, "Ori, go read with Zoë. Jasper, you read with Isabel." She said it in a way that made both boys obey her right away.

"Just for today, right?" Jasper said.

"Until I say so," Ms. Tosh said.

At least Jasper got to stay in the cozy Book Nook. Isabel came over and plopped down on the pillow beside him with her legs stretched out. She was a very freckly girl. She even had freckles on her legs.

"You read first, Jasper John," she said, smiling and showing the no-teeth space in her mouth.

Jasper's book was about a dog that could skateboard. As soon as he started reading, he was interested. Isabel was interested, too. Jasper knew she was interested because as he read, Isabel leaned in close to him. She leaned so close Jasper could smell her. She smelled like strawberries.

He thought she was trying to see the page he was reading. Maybe she needed glasses, because she leaned in close enough to —

"Yuck!" Jasper roared when he felt Isabel's wet tongue on his cheek. "Yuck!"

And Ms. Tosh said, "Jasper John Dooley! You've disrupted us enough for one day!"

Chapter 2

When Jasper John Dooley was the Star of the Week, everybody in the class wrote Compliments to him. Ms. Tosh stapled them all together in a book that Jasper took home with him. The Compliment at the end said: I love you, Jasper.

Back when Jasper was Star of the Week, he didn't know who had written the I-love-you Compliment. But now he knew. It must have been Isabel.

Jasper stayed away from Isabel for the rest of the day. After school, Mom was waiting to walk him and

Ori home. She always walked them home because Ori's mom was busy with Ori's baby sister. "How was your day?" she asked.

"Terrible," Jasper said. He was still wiping his cheek, trying to make the goopy feeling of being licked go away.

"Terrible? What happened?"

"Our reading buddies got changed," Ori said. "I'm not Jasper's reading buddy anymore."

"Come on," Jasper said. "Let's go."

They started walking.

"Who's your buddy now?" Mom asked Ori.

"Zoë."

"Who's yours, Jasper?" Mom asked.

"She's following us," Jasper said.

Mom looked back. Jasper had seen Isabel out

of the corner of his eye. Now he pretended to be walking like a monkey, bent over and scratching under his arms. That way he could secretly peek at Isabel from under his arm without her knowing. If Isabel saw him peeking at her, she would probably think he loved her, too.

Mom stopped and waited for Isabel to catch up. "I hear you're Jasper's new reading buddy."

"Yes," Isabel answered. "Today is the best day of my life!"

"Keep walking," Jasper said to Ori.

It was hard to walk like a bent-over monkey peeking under your own arm, but Jasper did it all the way to the corner of the schoolyard. All the way he watched Isabel smile at Mom without any front teeth and Mom smile back with teeth.

Luckily, he was too far away to hear what they were talking about.

"Today's the best day of Isabel's life," Ori said to Jasper. "She got to lick you."

Jasper looked around for a sword to slay his friend with.

"Now she's coming over with your mom," Ori said.

Jasper hid behind a telephone pole. When Mom and Isabel reached him, Isabel said to the telephone pole, "Bye, Jasper! See you tomorrow, Jasper!"

Then she ran away.

Mom laughed. She, Ori and Jasper crossed the street. At the alley, Ori waved and went home to his house. Jasper waved back. He was glad Ori hadn't told Mom that Isabel had licked him. He was so so so embarrassed.

At home, Mom made Jasper a snack. While she was cutting up carrot sticks, she told him, "Isabel invited you over for a playdate."

"A *what*?"

"You know what a playdate is. She asked for our phone number. So her mother could call. When I told it to her, she repeated it back until she memorized it. She said she'd remember it forever."

Mom was smiling while she told this to Jasper, the way she had smiled at Isabel while they were talking.

Jasper flopped down on the kitchen floor and groaned.

"Don't you think it would be fun to have a playdate with somebody besides Ori?"

"Ori is my best and closest friend. He lives just across the alley and one house down. If something so so so embarrassing happened to me at school, he wouldn't tell anybody about it. That means he's a good friend. And we're both knights."

"Can't Isabel be a knight?"

"No. She's a girl. All girls do is stay inside and brush their hair."

"Are you sure about that?" Mom asked. She put the carrot sticks on the table and went to the fridge for the dip.

"I mean when they're at home," Jasper said from the floor. "At school, they play babies."

"Well, I'm a girl. I do all kinds of things." She spooned the dip out into a little bowl.

"What things?" Jasper asked.

"There's your snack," Mom said. "I guess you think it got there all by itself."

Jasper sat up on the kitchen floor, but the phone started ringing, so he flopped down again. "Don't answer it!"

Mom stepped right over him and went to the phone.

"If it's about the playdate?" Jasper said. "Tell her I can't come."

"She'll want to know why," Mom said.

Jasper closed his eyes tight. "Tell her I'm sick."

But it wasn't Isabel or her mom calling. It was Jasper's Nan. Isabel's mom didn't call until after supper, when Jasper was in the basement scraping the dryer screen to get more lint for his collection. Jasper wasn't there to say "No, no, no, no!" to the playdate, so Mom went ahead and said "Yes."

That night Dad came into Jasper's room to say goodnight.

"I hear you have a playdate with a girl tomorrow," he said.

"I'm not going," Jasper said. "I feel sick."

Dad put his hand on Jasper's forehead. "You do feel hot."

"Do I?" Jasper said. "Oh, good!"

Dad asked him to stick out his tongue. He studied it, nodding and hmming. "Yes. I know what you've got."

"What?" Jasper asked.

"A terrible disease. Girl-itis. I used to get it a lot myself."

"I'm dying of it!" Jasper groaned. He rolled around on the bed clutching his stomach. "Agh! Rawr! Grrr!"

"I don't get it," he told Dad. "At school? All she ever does is tell on me. I'm not even her baby. I'm Zoë's baby. And now we have to have a playdate!"

Chapter 3

The next morning, Jasper got the lates for school and had to rush. He forgot all about the playdate. At recess and lunch, he was so busy playing knights with Ori and Leon in the bushes at the back of the schoolyard where Isabel couldn't find them that he didn't think about the playdate. After school, Mom was waiting, but when Jasper went over to her, Isabel came out of nowhere and grabbed his hand.

Jasper remembered the playdate then.

Mom was there to walk Ori home. Jasper had to go with Isabel! He kept his arms crossed tight so Isabel couldn't hold hands with him. As they walked, he looked over his shoulder and saw Mom and Ori walking in the opposite direction. He felt all watery inside, like he would never see them again.

Mom turned and waved. "Have fun!" she called.

Ori turned, too. He pretended he had a sword in his hand and was stabbing himself with it.

Isabel lived farther from school than Jasper and Ori did. The whole way she kept trying to make Jasper uncross his arms, pulling his wrist and tickling him, so she could hold his hand. She talked and talked.

"What do you want to do, Jasper? Are we going to play babies? We don't have to. We can play lots of things. We can play anything."

"Don't talk so much, Izzy," her mother said. "And don't pull on him like that. Can't you see you're scaring him?"

Isabel's mother didn't have any freckles. Also, she had all her teeth.

Isabel's house was about twice the size of Jasper's house. Isabel's dog was about a million times bigger than Jasper's, because Jasper didn't have a dog. It ran to the door to greet them, a huge black and brown dog that came up to Jasper's chin. Isabel hugged it and let it lick her freckly cheeks with its big slobbery tongue. Jasper finally uncrossed his arms so he could cover his face with his hands.

"This is Rollo. You can ride him. Get on, Jasper."

"No, thanks," Jasper said.

"Let's go upstairs."

Isabel rode down the hall on the back of the giant dog. Jasper followed, staying far enough behind that he wouldn't get clobbered by Rollo's big waggy tail. At the bottom of the stairs, Isabel said, "Sit, Rollo." The dog sat and she slid off his back. "Race you!" she screamed to Jasper just before she bolted up.

Isabel got to the top first.

"You had a head start," Jasper said.

"What do you want to do?" Isabel asked.

"Let's brush our hair," Jasper said. The sooner they finished brushing, the sooner he could go home and stop worrying about getting licked by Isabel or her dog.

Isabel seemed excited about hair brushing. She left Jasper in her room while she raced off for the brush.

Jasper was surprised that Isabel's room wasn't pink.

It was lots of colors, but what Jasper noticed most was the set of drums in the corner. There was even a stool to sit on while you played. He went over and tapped his fingers on a drum. Nothing.

"Your drums are broken," Jasper told Isabel when she came back with the brush and a big tube of something that looked like lime Jell-O toothpaste.

Isabel laughed. "You have to turn them on." She pressed a button. "Try it now."

Jasper picked a drumstick off the floor and tapped the cymbal. It made a soft *chunka* sound.

"Like this," Isabel said, attacking the drums with the hairbrush. The room filled with crashing and thumping. It sounded like the whole house was falling down.

"Izz-y!" Isabel's mother shouted from downstairs.

"Never mind," said Isabel. "Let's get brushing."

She dragged Jasper over to the bed and made him sit cross-legged while she knelt in front of him. She brushed his hair so hard Jasper squinched his eyes closed. Jasper felt something cold and wet on his head. "What's that?" he asked.

"Hair gel," Isabel said. "Turn this way."

Jasper turned his head. He saw right out her bedroom window into the backyard. "Is that a trampoline?" he asked.

"Yes. Now turn your head the other way."

When Isabel finished gelling Jasper, she sat back to look at him. She laughed so hard she toppled onto her side.

"What?" Jasper touched his head. It was covered with wet spikes.

Isabel handed him the brush. "Your turn now."

"Do I have to?"

"No. It's boring," Isabel said. "Let's do something else."

"Can we jump on the trampoline?" Jasper asked.

"Sure. Let's have a snack first."

This time Jasper was ready to race Isabel downstairs, but Isabel threw one leg over the banister and slid down faster than he could run. She beat him to the fridge, too. From the rack on the door, she took a jar of jam.

"Aren't we going to put it on bread or anything?" Jasper asked when she handed him a spoon from the drawer.

"Do you want some bread?"

"No. But what will your mom say?"

"She's working," Isabel said.

Through the kitchen door, Jasper could see Isabel's mom watching TV in the living room. He said, "She has a good job. My mom works in an office in our basement."

"That's not my mom," Isabel said. "That's Mandy, my nanny."

They sat on the floor and ate the jam out of the jar with spoons. Rollo came over. He seemed even bigger when they were on the floor, like a big, slobbery horse whose ears hung down. Isabel pushed him away.

"Look, Jasper." She smeared some jam on her lips. Jasper laughed.

"I'll put some on you, too," she said.

Then they went to the bathroom and looked in the mirror. Jasper's hair had hardened into spikes and his mouth was lipsticked with jam. He was a little disappointed that his hair wasn't green.

"Okay," he said. "Let's go jump."

When Mom came to pick up Jasper from his playdate, Jasper and Isabel were still jumping on the trampoline. Jasper couldn't stop. He loved the flip-floppy feeling in his stomach. He loved how, if he fell straight back — whee! — in a second he'd be on his feet again. Mom talked for a few minutes to Mandy, who was watching them from the back deck. Then Mom said, "Jasper. Time to go."

"No!"

"Yes. Your dad has supper ready."

Jasper climbed back down onto solid ground. It was boring. There was no spring to it.

"Say thank you to Isabel," Mom said.

"You're welcome, Jasper!" Isabel said, sliding off the trampoline and flinging herself at Jasper. He had to duck behind Mom.

"Can Jasper have a playdate tomorrow?" Isabel asked.

"Can I?" Jasper asked, and Mom laughed.

On the drive home, Mom kept looking at Jasper in the rearview mirror and smiling to herself. She didn't ask him about the playdate, not until later, when they were eating supper.

"So?" she said. "I noticed you weren't inside brushing your hair."

Jasper said, "She brushed mine, but I wouldn't brush hers."

Dad said, "Your hair sure looks different."

Jasper touched his head. At the back, it felt crunchy. The behind spikes had been flattened when he landed on his back on the trampoline. In front, he had three horns.

"And she put lipstick on me, too," Jasper complained. "Did you get her phone number?"

Mom smiled at Dad. "Jasper wants to go back tomorrow for another playdate."

"Tomorrow already? That's serious," Dad said. "What's she like, this Isabel?"

"She's covered in freckles and has no front teeth," Jasper said.

"Wow," Dad said. "She sounds gorgeous."

Chapter 4

The next day at school when the bell rang for recess, Jasper and Ori dashed out to look for swords. "Meet you out there, Leon!" they called to their dragon.

While they were looking for swords, Ori asked Jasper about his playdate. "So?" he said. "Did she lick you again?"

"No," Jasper said. "She has a trampoline. You should come over, too."

"No way," Ori said.

Jasper found a good sword. He slashed it around, then helped Ori look.

Isabel and Zoë pushed through the bushes. "There you are, you bad, bad babies!"

"We're not babies! We're knights!" Jasper cried, waving his sword at them. "Go away or we'll slay you."

Isabel nodded to Zoë, who was carrying something in the kangaroo pouch of her jacket. A whole jar of jam! Raspberry! Isabel waved two spoons.

Jasper looked at Ori.

"The thing is," Ori said. "No way."

"Yes way," the girls begged. "Play babies with us."

"My mom phoned your mom again," Isabel said to Jasper. "So we can have another playdate."

Even as Ori was scowling at him, even as Jasper

turned red from embarrassment, the feeling came
back. That soaring-through-the-air-stomach-flip-
floppy feeling. He loved that feeling! Last night,
he had tried to get it back by jumping on his bed. It
wasn't the same. Not at all.

"If we play babies with you now, will you leave us
alone at lunch?" Jasper asked.

"Yes," Isabel said.

"Promise?"

Isabel put her freckly hand over her heart. "Yes."

Jasper turned to Ori. "At lunch, we can use the jam
for dragon blood."

Ori liked this idea, so he threw down the stick
he'd found and said, "Wa-wa-wa-wa." He and Jasper
lay in the grass, kicking their arms and legs in the air.

Isabel rushed over and pulled Jasper onto her lap.

"Hey!" Zoë cried. "He's my baby!"

"I want to trade," Isabel said. She wrapped her arms tight around Jasper's chest.

Zoë said, "You don't trade babies. You keep the same baby all your life. Did your mom trade you?"

"Maybe," Isabel said.

Jasper tried to wriggle out of Isabel's arms, but she was a very strong girl. Zoë tugged as hard as she could on Jasper's ankles.

She couldn't pull him away from Isabel. Meanwhile, Ori lay on the ground wa-wa-waing.

His own mother didn't pay any attention to him.

"Help!" Jasper cried. "I'm stretching!"

Ori couldn't help because he was just a baby. The playground monitor couldn't help because she hardly ever came down to the back of the schoolyard where the bushes were.

Just then Leon showed up, and Jasper said, "Quick, Leon! Eat these girls!"

Leon flashed angry dragon eyes at the girls. He stuck out his claws and said, "Agh! Rawr! Grrr!"

The mothers blinked at Leon, then went right back to stretching Jasper.

The babies only got away from their bad mothers when the end-of-recess bell rang. Isabel let go, and Jasper and Ori ran all the way up to the classroom. They were supposed to take out their spelling books and copy the new words off the board. Jasper just sat there feeling stretched and wondering what to do about Isabel. He really wanted another playdate at Isabel's house so he could jump on her trampoline. If only Isabel didn't have to be there!

"Jasper?" Ms. Tosh said, coming over and tapping his spelling book so he would focus.

Jasper opened the book, but he still couldn't focus. He looked out the window. Somebody was walking past the school leading a horse.

"Rollo!" Isabel shrieked. She jumped up and ran to the window to wave.

"Isabel," Ms. Tosh said. "Will you please sit down?"

Chapter 5

Mom was a little late picking up Jasper and Ori from school that day. The boys had to stand around ignoring Isabel. She didn't make it easy. When they turned one way, showing Isabel their backs, she ran around so she was in their faces again, chattering away.

"Don't talk so much, Izzy," Mandy, her nanny, told her. "Can't you see you're scaring them? Let's go."

Finally, Mom showed up. "Sorry, boys. I have so much work this week I forgot the time."

"Hi, Jasper's mom!" Isabel said.

"Hello, Isabel. Tell your mother that Monday after school is fine."

"Jasper!" Isabel sang, jumping up and down and trying to hold his hand. "We're going to have another playdate!"

Jasper was so so so so embarrassed that she said that in front of Ori.

Then, as they were walking home, Mom made it worse. She said, "I'm not impressed with your manners, Jasper John Dooley. You were the one who wanted another playdate. Now you act like you don't even want to go."

"You don't want to go, do you?" Ori asked Jasper.

"She has a trampoline," Jasper reminded him.

"I think she's a great little girl," Mom said. "So full of energy."

"The thing is," Ori said, "she steals other people's babies. She had her own baby and she left him crying and hungry in the grass. Now he's an orphan. He doesn't feel very good about that."

"Is that you, Ori?" Mom asked.

Ori nodded and hung his head so he looked like a poor orphan nobody loved. Mom stopped to give him a hug.

"And I got stretched!" Jasper said. "Didn't you notice? I'm a lot taller."

"Oh, dear," Mom said. "Well, you have to go this time. If you don't want to go again, Jasper, you don't have to."

"Come to my house, Jasper," Ori said. "*I'm* your friend. I'm your *close* friend. Doesn't she live five streets away?"

Jasper felt his face turn the color of strawberry jam. Because he didn't want to go to Ori's house. Ori didn't have a trampoline.

Jasper got an idea. Why couldn't they buy a trampoline? If Jasper had his own trampoline, he wouldn't have to go to Isabel's house. And Ori could come over and jump, too.

He told Mom and Dad his idea after supper. They said a trampoline cost too much.

"I'll give you all the money I have." Jasper ran to his room to get his bank. When he pulled out the plug on the pig's stomach, three million dollars spilled onto the table.

"Now you have to count it," Mom said.

"Is that math?" Jasper asked.

"I guess it is," Mom said.

"No math!" Jasper said. "Anyway, I can tell just by looking at it that this is three million dollars. Isn't that enough?"

Dad spread Jasper's money around on the table. "A lot of this money is brown," he said. "So, no. It's not enough. Besides, you have a friend in the neighborhood who has a trampoline. Aren't you going to her house to jump on it?"

"I'd rather jump here," Jasper said.

"What difference does it make, jumping here or jumping there?"

"A lot! Here, I wouldn't have to jump with Isabel."

"Jasper John," Dad said. "Do you only like this freckly, toothless Isabel because she has a trampoline?"

"No," Jasper answered truthfully. "I don't like her at all."

Dad leaned back and laughed. He said to Mom, "Does that sound familiar, Gail?"

"Yes, it does, David." To Jasper, Mom said, "Your dad didn't like me either when he met me."

"Really?" Jasper asked Dad.

Dad nodded. "She had all her teeth, and I still didn't like her."

"He didn't like that I was smarter," Mom said.

"She actually is smarter," Dad told Jasper.

"Tell Jasper that I did more than stay inside and brush my hair," Mom said.

"She had messy hair," Dad said. "What this all means, Jasper, is that if you spend enough time with Isabel, you'll probably start to love her."

"Yuck!" Jasper cried. He ran out of the kitchen and all through the house waving his arms and yucking because the thought of loving Isabel was so horrible.

Chapter 6

The next week, Jasper and Ori started playing knights in a new way. First, Jasper was a knight chasing Leon the dragon and Ori was the lookout. He looked out for Isabel and Zoë and two other girls, Bernadette and Patty, who wanted to play babies now, too. If Ori saw the girls, he shouted to Jasper and Leon, who quickly moved to a new place. Then Ori took a turn being a knight and trying to slay Leon while Jasper looked out for the girls.

They even asked another boy in their class who

wasn't a knight, Paul C., to help. Paul C. always sat at a picnic table reading a book during recess and lunch. From the picnic table, he could watch what everybody was doing.

"If you see them sneaking up on us?" Jasper told Paul C. "Shout to us."

Paul C. nodded and pushed up his glasses.

This way the knights avoided being babies at both recess and lunch.

After lunch on Monday, they had reading time. When Ms. Tosh told everybody to sit with their reading buddies, Jasper rushed to Ori's table. He hoped that Ms. Tosh wouldn't remember that she had switched his buddy the week before.

"Ms. Tosh!" Isabel called out in a very loud voice. "Aren't I Jasper's reading buddy now? Didn't you say last time that we were buddies until you said so?"

Jasper started reading out loud with the book an inch from his face. He didn't chew the book. He read so so so fast and so so so well with his old reading buddy, Ori.

His old reading buddy, Ori, giggled. "Jasper's reading in fast forward," he said.

"Jasper, your reading buddy is Isabel. Please sit with her as you are supposed to." Ms. Tosh said this in a way that made Jasper obey her.

He dragged his feet all the way to the Book Nook at the back of room where Isabel was waiting for him with a big smile on her front-toothless face. He dropped down beside her. Leaning as far away as he could, he picked up a pillow and pressed it to his face so only his eyes showed. He started reading.

"I can't hear you, Jasper John," Isabel said. She squeezed in close, like she wanted to lick him.

Jasper pressed the pillow harder to his face.

Isabel put up her hand. "Ms. Tosh! Jasper still isn't being my buddy! He's being buddies with a pillow!"

Twice Isabel got Jasper in trouble! And he still had to go to her house for a playdate after school!

While he was at Isabel's house, a terrible thing happened. Isabel asked Jasper to marry her. She asked him while they were jumping on the trampoline. Jasper should have climbed down right then and phoned his mom to pick him up, but he was enjoying the trampoline flip-floppy feeling so so so so much.

Before they started jumping, they ate a whole jar

of cheese spread without bread while sitting on the kitchen floor. Then Jasper and Isabel drank two big glasses of water each. Now when they jumped there was a wonderful sloshing sound to go with the wonderful flip-floppy feeling in their stomachs.

Even though Isabel had let Rollo lick cheese spread off her spoon, then dipped it back in the jar and licked the next spoonful herself, and even though this had made Jasper feel like he might throw up, he stopped feeling sick once he was on the trampoline.

He didn't even feel like throwing up when Isabel asked him to marry her. He would have felt sick for sure if he'd been standing on the boring, unspringy ground.

He jumped high in the air after she asked him, twisted, then came back down with his back to her. Flip-flop-slosh-slosh went his stomach. He was waiting for an idea. If he waited long enough, one or two usually came along. Back up in the air he soared, his arms out like wings. Then he remembered something. He remembered when he was just a little kid and didn't understand about getting married.

"I can't get married to you," Jasper said. "I already promised to marry my mom."

"But Jasper," Isabel said, sticking out her bottom

lip so the toothless space didn't show. "I already told everybody that we were getting married."

Jasper got down off the trampoline then. Because now he thought he really would throw up.

"Who did you tell?" he asked.

Isabel was still jumping. "Zoë. And Bernadette and Patty. And Margo. And Leon."

"Not Ori?"

"I told Ori. I told Paul C." She went on naming names until she had named the whole class. "And I told Ms. Tosh. And I told Mrs. Kinoshita."

"You told the principal?" Jasper said. "When?"

"At lunch. We couldn't find you to play babies, so I went to see her in her office."

"What did she say?" Jasper asked.

"She said, 'Congratulations!'" Isabel somersaulted in midair.

"Hey!" Jasper said. "How did you do that? I want to try!"

"I'm never going over there again!" Jasper told Mom in the car on the way home from the playdate.

"Okay," Mom said. "But it looked to me like you were having a really good time. I had to ask you six times to get off that trampoline."

"I was doing flying somersaults! I just learned how. But those are the last flying somersaults I'll ever do until I have enough money to buy my own trampoline. Because I don't like Isabel. I don't like how she tells on me at school. I don't like how she ruins every game. I don't like how she lets her dog lick her spoon then licks it herself."

"Yuck!" Mom said. "Did she do that?"

"Yes!"

"And did you have to brush hair again?"

"That's the only good thing about her. She doesn't care about hair brushing."

"And she has a trampoline," Mom said.

Jasper nodded.

When they got home, Mom told Jasper she had something to show him. It was a little blue notebook. "For me?" Jasper asked.

"Sort of." Mom opened it, and Jasper saw that she had already written in it. She said, "Here are some of the things I did today when I wasn't brushing my hair."

Woke up Jasper

Made Jasper's breakfast

Called Jasper

Went to wake up Jasper again

Reminded Jasper to brush his hair

Picked up Jasper's towel from the floor

Flushed the toilet for Jasper

Made Jasper's lunch

Bought a notebook

Worked until 3:00

Picked up Jasper from his playdate

"Wow," Jasper said. "That's a lot of stuff."

"That's just today," Mom said. "The day isn't even finished yet."

"What's for supper?" Jasper asked.

Mom passed him the notebook and the pencil.

Jasper sat down and wrote:

Made supper for Jasper.

That night in bed, Jasper asked Dad, "Did Mom *make* you get married?"

"I guess she sort of did," Dad said. "We were together for a long time. Finally, she said I should marry her or find somebody else."

"So you had to?"

"I could have found somebody else, I guess. But like I said, it was too late. I already loved her."

After Dad turned out the light, Jasper lay awake worrying. How long? How long until it was too late for him? And could he NOT get married to Isabel and still jump on her trampoline?

Chapter 7

At lunchtime on Wednesday the boys were playing knights in their new way, behind the gym, with Jasper as the lookout. Jasper looked one way — no girls. He looked the other way — no girls. Then he turned to watch the terrible battle that was going on between Ori, the knight, and Leon, the dragon. But only for a minute. He had to keep looking out for the girls.

The next time Jasper turned to watch the battle, the dragon had managed to tear Ori's sword out of his hand. He broke it in three pieces. Now he crept toward Ori, flashing angry dragon eyes and roaring "Agh! Rawr! Grrr!" His claws reached for Ori, but instead of running away, Ori ran straight for the dragon and crashed into him. The dragon fell on his bum in the grass.

Ori used his next best weapon, his bare hands. Tickle-tickle! Tickle-tickle!

The dragon flopped down. Ori sat on his chest and let out a cheer.

At just that moment, just as Jasper was about to take his turn being a knight, two girls appeared. Zoë and Bernadette.

"Come on, Jasper! Let's go!"

"What?" Jasper cried as the girls grabbed him by the arms.

Ori and Leon jumped to their feet and rushed

over. "Leave him alone!" Ori yelled. He and Leon tickled the girls so they had to give up Jasper.

But more girls showed up. They swarmed Jasper and started dragging him toward the back of the schoolyard where the bushes were. Leon and Ori tried to free Jasper by tickling all the girls, but there were just too many. As soon as one girl let go, another grabbed Jasper instead. It seemed like every girl from their class was there trying to steal Jasper. But Jasper noticed that one girl was missing.

And here she came. Jasper froze when he saw her. So did Ori and Leon.

Isabel was coming toward them with a crown of dandelions in her hair. She was riding on Rollo.

"Izzy!" Mandy called across the schoolyard. "I brought your lunch! Rollo can't run in the playground! Dogs aren't allowed at school!"

"Giddy up, Rollo," Isabel said, and the dog began to bound toward the group of kids. Isabel held tight to his collar. The other girls all cheered and clapped. They weren't afraid of Rollo.

Leon was. He turned and ran into the gym.

Ori stepped in front of Jasper. "I'll protect you," he said.

Just then Rollo stopped so suddenly Isabel nearly flew off his back. He'd found something to sniff. He pushed his big snout into the grass and turned so that his back was to Ori and Jasper. Whatever Rollo smelled made him so happy that his big waggy tail began slashing back and forth.

Thwunk!

It knocked Ori over. While he was still on the

ground wondering what had hit him, Isabel jumped off Rollo's back.

Mandy arrived. "Are you all right?" she asked Ori, who nodded and sat up.

"Your mother isn't going to be very happy when she hears about this," Mandy told Isabel. Isabel didn't answer. She was already leading Jasper away with the rest of the girls.

"Heel, Rollo," Mandy said, taking the dog by the leash and leading him away like Jasper, but in the other direction.

The swarm of girls and Jasper passed Paul C. sitting at a picnic table. "Paul C.!" Jasper cried. "Help me!"

Paul C. looked up from his book, but he couldn't do anything.

The girls dragged Jasper all the way to the bushes at the back of the schoolyard where the playground monitor hardly ever went. "Stand beside me," Isabel told Jasper. "Stop wiggling." She wrapped her arm tight around Jasper's arm.

"Ouch!" he said.

She was a very strong girl. A strong, freckled girl with a dandelion crown drooping on her head.

Zoë stood in front of them, her hands pressed together like a book. She opened the book. Some of the other girls were giggling. Some were stripping leaves off the bushes and tossing them in the air so they fluttered down on Isabel and Jasper.

"What am I supposed to say?" Zoë asked Isabel.

"Say I love Jasper. Say we're getting married. And then ask Jasper if he takes me for his wife. That's

what they say on TV. Jasper? When she says that? You have to say, 'I do.'" She jabbed him with her freckly elbow.

Jasper frowned.

"Jasper," Zoë said. "Isabel loves you. She never stops talking about you. Do you take her for your wife?"

He stood in the circle of girls, waiting for an idea. Hurry, hurry, he thought.

Isabel elbowed him again, and just then Jasper's knees gave out. He fell to the ground, almost pulling Isabel down with him.

"Wa-wa-wa-wa!" he cried, waving his arms and legs in the air. "Wa-wa-wa-wa!"

And then the bell rang.

Chapter 8

After school, Mom talked to Mandy for a long time while Jasper and Ori waited at the corner of the schoolyard. Isabel didn't come over. She couldn't because Mandy was holding on to the collar of her shirt. Every time Isabel tried to sneak away, Mandy yanked her back.

"Do you want to come to my house?" Ori asked Jasper.

Jasper did, but he was afraid that Ori would ask about what had happened after Rollo knocked Ori over with his tail. Then he remembered it was Wednesday. On Wednesday Jasper always visited his Nan.

That's what he told Ori. "I have to go see my Nan. I'll come to your house tomorrow."

"Did they make you play babies?" Ori asked.

"Yes!" Jasper lied.

"So all those girls are your mothers now?"

Jasper nodded. He would rather they be his mothers than be married to them!

Ori hung his head like a sad orphan nobody loved.

Jasper's Nan lived in an apartment not far from Jasper's house. On Wednesdays, when Jasper visited, they did so so many fun things together. They rode up and down the elevator making horrible faces in the mirrors on the walls. They played Go Fish for jujubes. They played Dress Up Nan.

Mom dropped Jasper off but didn't go in like she usually did. Nan was waiting for him in the jungly lobby.

"Your mom has a lot of work this week," Nan said.

Jasper nodded. "And now she's writing a book, too."

"She is?" Nan said. "She didn't tell me that."

Nan remembered to let Jasper press the elevator button. She always remembered. As soon as they started going up, Nan pulled back her lips so all her teeth showed. She looked so so so ugly. When she was a girl a long time ago, the dentists weren't very good.

"Yuck!" Jasper said.

Now Jasper turned to face the mirror. He tucked in
his chin and puffed his cheeks and crossed his eyes.

"Stop!" Nan cried. "You win!"

When they reached Nan's floor, Jasper pressed
the button again. They rode right back down,
making more horrible faces. Jasper won every
contest except the last one, when Nan used her

glasses. She smiled so that her cheeks lifted up. Then she pushed the frames of her glasses into the pillows of her cheeks. This made her eyes stretch down. She looked so so so so ugly!

Before they played Dress Up Nan and Go Fish for jujubes, Nan made Jasper a snack. She made him toast fingers and a soft-boiled egg. Jasper was allowed to put as much pepper on his egg as he wanted. He put so much on that it looked like he was dipping his toast fingers in dirt.

"I hear you have a new friend at school," Nan said.

Jasper stubbed his toast finger in his cup of dirt, frowning.

Nan laughed. "That's an ugly face! You must really like her!"

"I don't!"

Nan loved to tell Jasper stories about when she was young. Today she told him about when she was a girl at school. "In art class, we used to draw with nib pens. Nib pens are pens you dip in ink. The ink came in bottles. Do you know how a girl knew that a boy liked her?"

"No," Jasper said.

"When he dipped the ends of her pigtails in ink during art."

"Did you get your pigtails dipped?" Jasper asked, dipping another toast finger.

"All the time. It made me so mad. I never liked those boys. I only liked the quiet boys who minded their own business. Of course, those boys never liked me. What's the name of the girl you don't like?"

Jasper said, "Isabel."

"What don't you like about her?"

"She's too rough. I like playing quiet games like knights. I mind my own business with my friends at recess and lunch. I look for dragons."

Nan nodded. "You're just the kind of boy for me."

Later, after Dress Up Nan and Go Fish, Mom came to pick up Jasper. She rapped the jaws of Nan's lion's head knocker. When Jasper and Nan opened the door, Mom was standing in the hall writing in the little blue notebook.

"That's the book I was telling you about, Nan," Jasper said. "The one Mom's writing."

"Oh, I see!" Nan said, laughing. "What's it about?"

Mom finished writing and turned the book around to show them. It said:

Picked up Jasper from Nan's

Jasper read what was written just above that:

Set up playdate with Isabel

"What?!" Jasper cried. "I don't want any more playdates with her!"

Mom said, "I know you said that, but you looked like you were having so much fun."

"I like her trampoline," Jasper said. But he didn't like it enough to marry Isabel. "I don't want to go over there ever again."

"That's okay, then," Mom said. "Because Isabel is coming to our house."

Chapter 9

Every Thursday at school, the Star of the Week presented his or her talent. Margo was the Star that week, and her talent was crocheting potholders. She stood at the front of the class pulling potholder after potholder out of a big bag. She passed them around. All the potholders were orange.

"This is the first one I made. As you can see, it's not very square," Margo said. "Now I'm going to show you how I crochet a potholder. When I finish, I'm going to ask you which potholder is your favorite."

Out of the bag came a ball of orange wool and a stick with a hook on the end. Margo tied a loop at the end of the ball of wool and attached it to the stick. She wiggled the stick around.

Jasper couldn't really see what she was doing because his table was at the back of the classroom. Anyway, it didn't seem interesting. When Jasper was the Star of the Week, he'd drunk a lot of water and jumped around making sloshing music with his stomach. As soon as he thought of that, he remembered the trampoline and the soaring-through-the-air-stomach-flip-floppy feeling that he loved and would never feel again. Not until he saved three million dollars. It made him so sad and watery that when somebody passed him a potholder, he used it to wipe his eyes.

"Does anybody have a question for Margo?" Ms. Tosh asked.

"I haven't finished crocheting my potholder," Margo said.

"I think we'll have question time while you are crocheting, Margo. Otherwise it will take too long."

Isabel's hand shot in the air.

Ms. Tosh said, "Isabel, did you have a question for Margo?"

"I just wanted to say that I have a playdate with Jasper John after school today. I'm going to his house. He came to my house twice, and now I'm going to his."

Jasper slithered down as far as he could in his chair. He piled three potholders on his face.

"Thank you for that information, Isabel. But now we're talking about Margo's talent."

Ori, at the table next to Jasper's, whispered across to him, "I thought you were coming to my house!"

Jasper tore the potholders off his face. "I want to come to your house! I didn't ask her for a playdate! My mom did. She said I had to invite her because I went to her house twice."

"You're in love," Ori sniffed.

"I'm not!" Jasper said.

"And the thing is? You used to be a knight."

Ms. Tosh said, "Can the boys at the back of the room please stop whispering?"

Everybody in the class thought Jasper and Isabel were going to get married. Half the class, all the girls, had seen them almost get married. Now everybody in the class knew that Isabel was coming to Jasper's house after school. They probably thought that Jasper would get married to Isabel then.

During math, Jasper spent most of his time making a sign. It looked like this:

He would have to get home first, before Isabel, and tape the sign to his door.

Because he was making his sign, Jasper didn't finish his math worksheet. Ms. Tosh made him stay in at recess until it was done. By the time he got outside, recess was half over. He had to run all over the playground looking for Leon and Ori, who were playing knights somewhere where the girls couldn't find them. When Jasper finally spotted them on the hopscotch court, he got a big surprise.

Ori was the dragon. Leon was chasing him around waving a stick. Leon was always the dragon because he was the best at being dead. But now he was a knight. And so was Paul C.

"Paul C.?" Jasper said. "What are you doing here?"

"What are *you* doing here, Jasper?" Paul C. asked. "I thought you were playing babies with the girls."

"I wasn't!" Jasper cried. "I was finishing my math!"

"That math was so easy," Paul C. said, waving his stick and running off.

Easy for Paul C.! Jasper ran with him, because he was chasing Ori. "Ori!" Jasper called. "I can play, too, right? I'm still a knight, right?"

"Agh! Rawr! Grrr!" Ori said, running right past Jasper.

And then the bell rang.

Chapter 10

Jasper was so so so so mad at Isabel. So so so so so so mad! He came out of school at the end of the day, and instead of going over to where Mom stood with Isabel and Ori, he stomped ahead to the corner of the schoolyard and waited there with his arms crossed tight.

Isabel skipped along beside Mom and Ori. She chattered away. "You're not coming to Jasper John's house, too, are you, Ori? I thought it was just me and Jasper. I like to have Jasper all to myself. We do lots of things."

"What things?" Ori asked.

"Jasper really liked it when I brushed his hair," she said. "I put lipstick on him, too."

Mom said, "Did you want to come over, Ori? I think Jasper would really like that."

"The thing is, I don't like hair brushing or putting on lipstick," Ori said. "So, no thank you."

Jasper couldn't even look at Ori. He was so so so so so embarrassed.

"Jasper," Mom said. "Why did you go ahead like that?"

Jasper didn't answer.

"Jasper?" Mom said. "Hello?"

"Agh! Rawr! Grrr!" Jasper said.

Isabel laughed and laughed, showing the empty space in her mouth. Then she tried to take Jasper's hand. He stuffed both of them under his arms and turned away.

They all crossed the street together — Mom, Jasper, Ori and Isabel.

"What are we going to do at your house, Jasper? We can play babies. We can play with your toys," Isabel chattered. "We can brush hair again. I think it's boring, but I'll do it because you like it."

Ori turned and headed down the alley to his house. He didn't say good-bye, and neither did Jasper.

Mom said, "My goodness, Isabel. These boys seem really grumpy."

"They're always like that," Isabel said. "I'm used to it."

Jasper remembered his sign then and bolted ahead to get home first. But the door was locked, so he couldn't go in and get the tape. Instead, he took the sign out of his backpack, uncrumpled it and stood by the door holding it up.

Mom and Isabel arrived a few minutes later. When Isabel saw Jasper's sign, she clapped her hands. "Is that a picture of me, Jasper? Can I keep it? I want to keep it. I'll put it on my wall."

Mom didn't like the sign as much as Isabel. She unlocked the door and asked Isabel to go ahead inside and make herself at home. "Jasper will be right there," she said. She closed the door again and crossed her arms the way Jasper had crossed his before he needed them to hold up the sign.

"Jasper John Dooley," Mom said. "Isabel is your guest. You will be as nice to her as she was to you when you were a guest at her house. Do you understand?"

"I don't like her!" Jasper said. "Dad said I would start to like her more and more, but I don't. I like her less and less. I'm not a knight anymore because of Isabel! Paul C. took my place, Mom. Paul C.!"

"That's no reason not to have good manners. If you don't make her welcome, you can forget about ever getting a trampoline for your birthday," Mom said.

After she said that, she turned the color of jam.

"Am I getting a trampoline for my birthday?" Jasper asked.

Mom said, "That depends."

Suddenly Jasper liked Isabel. He liked her a lot! Because if he had never gone over to her house, he would never have jumped on a trampoline and felt that soaring-through-the-air-stomach-flip-floppy feeling that was the best feeling he'd ever had.

And if he had never had that feeling, he would never have asked for a trampoline, which he didn't have to save three million dollars for anymore. All because of Isabel! He just had to be nice to her until Mandy came to pick her up!

He threw himself at Mom and hugged her. "I love you so so so so much!"

That was a good feeling, too. The flip-floppy-I-really-love-you feeling he felt right then.

"Thank you," Mom said, laughing.

Jasper burst inside. "Isabel? Where are you?"

Isabel was in the living room jumping on the sofa.

"Oh," Jasper said. "I don't think you should do that. It's not allowed."

"I jump on the sofa at my house," Isabel said, jumping even higher.

"You should stop before my mom sees you. Let's go to my room and jump on the bed."

"Okay!" Isabel yelled. She took a flying leap over the side table, almost knocking the lamp to the floor.

In Jasper's room, Isabel ran all around looking at everything. "Is this your desk?" she asked.

Jasper wondered who else's desk it could be. It was in *his* room. Before he could say this, Isabel dashed to his bookshelf and started pulling out books and lifting down his soccer trophies.

"What's this, Jasper? What's in this box?" Isabel asked, grabbing his lint collection off the shelf.

"Careful with that!"

Jasper lunged for the box and took it from her before she spilled out his lint.

"What is it? What is it? What is it?" she asked.

Jasper was surprised she didn't know. He'd brought his lint collection to school when he was Star of the Week. Now he took it over to the bed. Isabel sat beside him and watched as he carefully unlatched the lid.

"Oh, right!" Isabel said. "I remember."

His Nan had given this box to him. It was a jewelry box, but Jasper wasn't using it for jewelry. It was for lint.

The biggest compartments in the jewelry box were packed with plain gray dryer lint. Lint with colored flecks went in another compartment. There was a compartment for pocket lint, too, and a very special compartment that had only a tiny bit of lint in it. That kind of lint was rare and hard to collect. It was belly-button lint. The only place Jasper could get belly-button lint was from his dad.

Jasper explained all this again to Isabel. She seemed interested because, as he explained the different compartments, she gasped.

But she wasn't gasping. She was taking a huge gulp of air. With the huge gulp of air puffing out her cheeks, she leaned over his lint collection.

"No!"

Jasper slammed the lid closed before she could blow all the lint out of the box.

He pulled his desk chair over to his bookshelf and stood on it so he could put his collection on the top shelf. He was so so so so mad again.

"Okay! Let's jump!" Isabel said, standing on the bed.

Jasper remembered the trampoline he was going to get for his birthday if he was nice to Isabel until her nanny picked her up. When he remembered, he wasn't mad anymore. He jumped on the bed with Isabel until she said, "This is boring."

"What do you want to do instead?" Jasper asked.

"Let's wrestle!"

"Hey!" Jasper cried as Isabel pulled him down by the leg.

She sat on his back and bounced up and down,

making the air *pfft-pfft-pfft* out of him and not come back in. Jasper knew then that he would never get a trampoline. *Pfft-pfft-pfft!* He would never get a trampoline because he couldn't — *pfft-pfft-pfft!* — be nice to Isabel until her nanny picked her up.

He'd be dead by then.

Jasper thought of Ms. Tosh. How did she keep not only Isabel but all the kids in the class from throwing books on the floor and bouncing on each other?

She did it by talking to them in a voice they had to obey.

"Isabel!" Jasper said. "You've disrupted us enough for one day!"

And Isabel stopped.

Jasper sat up and breathed some air. What else?

What else did Ms. Tosh do to keep control?

She gave seatwork.

Jasper pointed to the chair. "Isabel? Will you please sit down?"

Isabel sat on the chair. Jasper got up and cleared space on his desk, which was piled with toys. On the bookshelf, he found some puzzle books. "Here. Do this page."

He tapped the book twice with his finger, the way Ms. Tosh did, so that Isabel would focus.

"Okay," she said. "Do you have a pencil?"

Jasper couldn't find a pencil anywhere. "You stay in your seat, Isabel," he said, backing out of the room.

"I will," Isabel promised.

He ran to the kitchen, where there were pens in a

jar by the phone. He was surprised that Isabel was still in the chair when he got back. She took the pen and started on the crossword puzzle. Jasper opened another puzzle book and sat on the bed to connect the dots.

"Done!" Isabel sang before Jasper had even connected half the dots.

He got up to check her work. Isabel had filled the little squares like this:

Isabel asked, "Do you know what *X* and *O* mean, Jasper?"

"No," Jasper said.

"*X* is a kiss. *O* is a hug."

"What letter is a lick?" Jasper asked.

"A lick?" Isabel laughed. "Jasper John, you're so funny!" She snatched Jasper's puzzle book out of his hand. "Connect-the-dots! I love connect-the-dots! Connect my dots, Jasper."

She held out her arm.

"Okay," Jasper said.

They sat on the floor together. Jasper put the tip of his pen on one freckle and drew a straight line to another. He had no idea what he was drawing. He was just connecting Isabel's dots. Soon he saw a picture coming.

"A sailboat!" Isabel sang. "You're good at drawing, Jasper. Draw a dog on this arm. Draw Rollo."

She held out her other arm and Jasper connected the dots to make a dog.

Isabel laughed. Jasper laughed. Then Isabel stretched out on the floor so Jasper could connect more of her dots. She had so so so many dots on her stomach.

The doorbell rang. Mom didn't hear it from the basement, so Jasper went to answer it. Isabel followed him.

"Where's your mom?" she asked.

"She's working."

"What does she do?"

"Right now she's writing a book," Jasper said.

"A book! What kind of book? A kids' book?"

"A small, blue book."

Jasper opened the door. It was Mandy. "Already?" he said.

"It's five thirty," Mandy said. Then she turned to Isabel. "Izzy! Look at you! Your mother isn't going to be very happy. You'd better have a bath as soon as you get home."

"Do you want to have a playdate tomorrow, Jasper?" Isabel asked him. "This was fun!"

Jasper laughed because she looked so so so funny with a cat on her forehead and its tail hanging down her nose. There was a flower on one cheek and a bird on the other. Her arms and legs were doodle pads. And so was her stomach under her shirt.

Chapter 11

The next day Isabel got the lates. The kids were all at their tables writing Compliments to Margo and eating the cupcakes she had brought when somebody knocked on the door. Ms. Tosh answered it. Jasper saw Mandy in the hall. Ms. Tosh stepped out and closed the door. A few minutes later she came back inside with Isabel. Ms. Tosh had her arm around Isabel the way she put her arm around a kid coming back from the sickroom.

Everybody stared at Isabel. Ms. Tosh put a finger to her lips.

All the kids nodded and went back to writing Compliments to Margo just as if Isabel had not come in late with connect-the-dot drawings all over her face.

The Star, Margo, got to do anything she wanted while the rest of the class was writing Compliments to her. She was playing with Hammy, the little brown hamster in the cage at the back of the room. She didn't see Ms. Tosh put her finger to her lips. Now she turned and saw Isabel. In a very loud voice, she cried out, "Isabel! What happened?"

"Jasper John did this to me!" Isabel told the class. "He connected all my dots when I was at his house yesterday! Look!"

She pulled up her shirt to show her stomach. She pulled up her long sleeves and the legs of her pants. Everybody saw how Jasper had turned her into a connect-the-dots doodle pad.

"Didn't you have a bath?" Jasper asked.

"I had three baths," Isabel said. "This is permanent marker. Do you know what 'permanent' means?"

"Forever?" Jasper said.

"It means I'm going to have a cat on my forehead for the rest of my life!"

Leon said, "I like how the tail is hanging down your nose."

"It looks terrible!" Isabel roared. "I'm not allowed to play with you ever again, Jasper John. My mom is going to phone your mom. She's really mad."

Jasper slithered down in his desk. He wished he had some potholders to cover his face.

"Isabel," Ms. Tosh said. "Please sit down. We're writing Compliments to Margo."

When Isabel's mom phoned Jasper's mom, Jasper's mom would change her mind about getting him a trampoline for his birthday. Jasper felt sad about that. But he felt better in the lunchroom with Ori and Leon and Paul C., because Paul C. said, "I guess those girls won't be bothering you anymore. I guess you're going to be a knight again."

Being a knight with his friends was better than having a trampoline. Jasper knew that now.

Paul C. took off his glasses and cleaned them. He looked just as sad as Jasper had felt a moment ago.

"You can be a knight, too," Jasper told him.

"Can I?" Paul C.'s face lit up. "Look," he said, turning over the book he had brought down to the lunchroom. It was about knights. The boys leafed through it while they were eating. It gave them some good ideas about shields.

As soon as they finished eating, they rushed outside to play.

They were eenie-meenie-miney-moeing to see who would be the dragon when Isabel pushed through the bushes. "Come on, Jasper," she said in a voice that was hard not to obey.

"Where?" Jasper asked.

"You have to get married to me. Nobody else will now that you drew all over my face."

Jasper stood up. He could see all the girls on the other side of the bushes waiting with crossed arms. Isabel crossed her arms, too. She wiggled her nose. The cat's tail twitched. That cat was so so so so mad!

"In case you're wondering, I still love you," she said. "I just don't like you anymore."

Jasper's stomach flip-flopped, but not in a nice way. Isabel was going to make Jasper get married to her, and there was nothing he could do about it. Jasper started to go with Isabel. He had to.

But just then Paul C. sprang up and rushed at Isabel with the book about knights in his hands. Isabel looked surprised because usually Paul C. was so quiet and just sat by himself at the picnic table minding his own business.

Paul C. turned the book sideways and opened and closed it in front of his face. The book opening and closing looked just like the horrible snapping jaws of a dragon, jaws that came closer and closer to Isabel.

"I'm going to bite you," the dragon said in a quiet voice that was twice as scary as a roar.

"Ah!" Isabel yelled. "I'm telling on you, Paul C.! I'm going to find the monitor! You're in big trouble! Biting isn't allowed!"

Chapter 12

Jasper invited Ori, Paul C. and Leon to his house after school. Leon couldn't come because he had a piano lesson. Paul C. was allowed even though he had spent part of lunch in the principal's office where he had never been in his whole life. He had to go to the principal's office because what he'd done to Isabel was Very Dangerous.

"You had to go to the principal's office?" Paul C.'s mother asked after school.

"It's Very Dangerous to scare people with a book about knights," Paul C. said.

"He was protecting his friend," Ori told her.

"Me!" Jasper said.

And Paul C.'s mom looked so so so so happy. She said to Jasper's mom, "Paul is new to this school. I'm so glad he's found friends."

Ori and Paul C. came to Jasper's house to make a plan. Their plan was about how to make Isabel NOT in love with Jasper. Jasper had tried ignoring her. He had tried being nice. The only thing he hadn't tried was pretending to love her, too.

"Girls like quiet boys who mind their own business. That's why she loves me. Girls don't like boys who dip their pigtails in ink," Jasper explained.

"The thing is," Ori said, "I don't know what you're talking about."

"My Nan told me," Jasper said.

But at Jasper's school, they didn't draw with nib pens in art class. They mostly used colored pencils.

"Mom!" Jasper called.

Mom came and the boys asked her, "Would you like it if a boy dipped your hair in jam?"

"In jam? No," she said. "I'd be really mad."

"What about if he did this?" Paul C. asked. He smiled so that his cheeks lifted up. Then he pushed the frames of his glasses into his cheeks so his eyes stretched down. He looked so so so ugly!

"Stop it, Paul!" Mom said. "You're scaring me!"

The boys smiled evil smiles.

And Mom took the little blue notebook out of her pocket and wrote something down.

At breakfast on Monday, Jasper asked for toast.

"Toast?" Dad said. "You always have cereal. Is something wrong?"

Jasper said, "I feel toasty."

While the toast was toasting, Jasper took the jam from the fridge. He did a test with his own hair. He had to hold the jar against the side of his head because his hair was too short to dip.

"Jasper?" Dad asked. "What are you doing with the jam?"

Jasper took the jar away. "Is there jam on my hair?"

"Just a little. Are you okay, Jasper?"

"The jam's too thick," Jasper said. "How can I make it more like ink?"

"Like ink?" Dad said. "Well, you could add water."

While Jasper was at the kitchen sink stirring water into the jam, Dad used a wet cloth to wipe the jam out of Jasper's hair. He went to put the cloth in the laundry hamper. When he came back, Jasper was sitting at the table pouring out cereal for himself.

"I thought you were having toast," Dad said.

"The jam was too watery."

"You seem funny this morning, Jasper," Dad said. He put a hand on Jasper's forehead. "Uh-oh. It's not what I think it is, is it?"

Jasper nodded.

Girl-itis!

At school, Ms. Tosh noticed right away that Jasper had got new glasses. She didn't notice that Paul C. didn't have glasses anymore.

"I still can't see very well," Jasper told her. "I need to move closer to the board."

"Go to the seat where you would see best, Jasper," Ms. Tosh said.

Jasper didn't need to pretend he was having trouble seeing. He had to wave his arms in front of himself as he walked so he wouldn't crash into anything. How could Paul C. be so good at math when everything was so blurry?

Jasper stopped at Margo and Bernadette's table. He looked over the top of the glasses to make sure it was the right place. "I need to sit here, behind Isabel," he told Ms. Tosh.

Margo and Jasper switched places. As soon as Jasper was seated behind Isabel, he squinted at the back of her head through Paul C.'s glasses. Paul C.'s glasses were junk! Jasper couldn't even see Isabel's pigtails!

He slid the glasses down and looked at Isabel over the top of them.

Isabel didn't have pigtails. Her hair barely reached her shoulders. Dipping her hair was going to be harder than he thought.

Jasper decided to skip ahead to the next part of the plan. He tapped Isabel's shoulder. When she turned around, Jasper pushed the frames of Paul C.'s glasses into his smiling cheeks so that his eyes stretched down.

Instead of screaming, Isabel laughed. "Jasper John, I'm so happy you're sitting behind me now. Did you notice? The cat is almost gone?" She pointed to the ghost of the connect-the-dots cat on her forehead. The tail had completely vanished.

"I took eleven baths on the weekend," she said.

"Meet me in the bushes at recess," Jasper whispered, lifting the glasses frames.

"Okay. Can we get married then?"

"Maybe," Jasper said. "But don't bring any other girls with you."

"Isabel and Jasper?" Ms. Tosh said. "Please stop whispering."

At recess, Jasper waited behind the bushes at the back of the schoolyard where the playground monitor hardly ever went. Ori, Leon and Paul C. were crouched on the other side waiting for Isabel, too.

She came alone. "Here you are, Jasper John!" She sounded so happy to see him. But she wouldn't be happy for long.

"Let's get married!" she said.

"First, I have to do something," Jasper said.

"What?" Isabel asked. "What? What? What?"

Jasper blew two raspberries, which was the signal for the other boys to jump out from behind the bushes with the jam and grab hold of Isabel. She shrieked in surprise.

"What are we going to do now?" she asked in an unterrified voice.

"I'm going to dip your hair in jam!" Jasper shouted. He laughed an evil laugh — "Ha ha ha ha!" — as he came toward her, unscrewing the lid.

Isabel tilted her head so it would be easier for Jasper to get her hair in the jar. Jasper circled her, cackling and dipping. Isabel cackled, too. He dipped the sides and the back. Her bangs were too short to dip. When he finished dipping, he stepped back to look at Isabel. Runny jam dripped off the ends of her hair. Her shoulders were soaked with it.

Isabel ripped her arms free from Ori and Paul C.'s grip. She snatched the jar.

"Ha ha ha ha!" she said, dumping the jam over Jasper's head.

Chapter 13

Isabel thought it was wonderful to sit in the hall on a piece of newspaper with Jasper. The newspaper was because they were dripping with jam. Everybody who walked by stopped and said, "Oh, my goodness! What happened? Call an ambulance!"

And every time Isabel crowed out, "It's not blood! It's jam! Ha ha ha ha!"

Jasper did not think it was wonderful. He thought it was sticky and embarrassing. His shirt was pasted to his body with jam. Yuck! Sharing the newspaper meant he had to sit right up against sticky Isabel. Yuck! And Isabel kept leaning even closer to him with her tongue out, trying to lick the jam off his face.

"Yuck, yuck, yuck!"

Finally, Mrs. Kinoshita came. She stared down at them with crossed arms. "To the bathroom. Now. Clean yourselves up. Don't jam up my office."

Isabel and Jasper obeyed her right away.

When they got back from the bathroom, Isabel ran straight to the big chair in Mrs. Kinoshita's office, the one across from her desk. She climbed up in it and swung her feet. She loved the office! She'd been there so so many times.

"Welcome back, Isabel," Mrs. Kinoshita said. "Hello, Jasper."

"Sit beside me, Jasper John," Isabel said, patting the

place beside her. "There's lots of room."

The times Jasper had been to the office he had tried not to sit in that chair. He didn't like it when his feet didn't touch the ground. He told Isabel, "I prefer to stand."

Mrs. Kinoshita folded her hands on her desk. She liked to get to the bottom of things. "So what happened out there?"

"Jasper asked me to get married at recess," Isabel said, pushing her wet hair off her face.

"I did not!" Jasper said.

"Then why did you want me to meet you behind the bushes?"

"So I could dip your hair in jam."

"And why did you want to do that, Jasper?" Mrs. Kinoshita asked.

Isabel answered. "I guess he likes girls with red hair. And I like boys with red hair. That's why I dumped the jam on him."

"She came into the boys' bathroom to clean up," Jasper said.

"Isabel," Mrs. Kinoshita said. "I told you not to do that anymore."

"I just wanted to be with Jasper," Isabel said. "Are you going to make us stay in at lunch? Can we stay in together? We were both bad together so I think we should stay in together."

"We weren't bad together," Jasper said. "First I was bad, then you were."

"Staying together would be more of a reward than a punishment, Isabel," Mrs. Kinoshita said. "You will stay in separately. After you finish eating lunch, Jasper will go to the classroom. Isabel, you will come here and sit with me."

Isabel stuck her bottom lip over her toothless place.

"And before you go back to your class, both of you need to choose a clean top out of the Lost and Found."

"Jasper!" Isabel sang. "We get to play Dress Up!"

Jasper tucked in his chin and crossed his eyes.

He asked, "Can I have my jam back?"

Dad was waiting for Jasper and Ori after school.

Jasper came running. "Where's Mom?"

"I came home early. You'll never guess what I found."

"What?" Jasper asked.

"Mom. Asleep on the sofa. She's had a hard few weeks, you know."

"I know," Jasper said.

"Jasper had a hard few weeks, too," Ori said. "But his life is going to be so much easier now!"

They all walked home — Dad, Jasper and Ori.

"Explain," Dad said.

Jasper said, "I had to stay in at lunch."

"Because he dipped Isabel's hair in jam," Ori said.

"Is that what you wanted that jam for, Jasper?" Dad asked.

"Yes. To make her NOT in love with me. But it didn't work. It just made me sticky. It just made her love me more."

"The thing is," Ori said, "she tried to lick him again."

"Then at lunch, something happened. I was eating with Ori and Leon and Paul C. Isabel was eating at the next table. With Zoë and Margo and Bernadette."

"I had pudding in my lunch," Ori said. "Vanilla."

"He doesn't like vanilla," Jasper said.

They stopped at the alley where Ori always turned to go to his own house. "What does this have to do with Jasper's life getting easier?" Dad asked.

"There was some jam left. So I gave it to Ori to put in his pudding. To make it strawberry."

"It was good!" Ori said.

"So I asked to taste it," Jasper said. "And it was. So so so so good! Then Leon wanted to try it and Paul C., too."

"And then Jasper's life got much easier!" Ori said. "Because Isabel saw. She saw us sharing a spoon. And she stood up and shouted 'Yuck!' across the lunchroom. She said, 'I'm going to the principal's office anyway. I'm going to tell her what you did. Then I'm going to ask her if I can lie down in the nurse's room because I think I'm going to throw up!'"

Dad laughed and laughed.

"Then, after lunch? It was reading time," Ori said. "Isabel asked Ms. Tosh if we could go back to our old reading buddies. She said she didn't want to be buddies with Jasper anymore."

"Ori's my reading buddy again!" Jasper sang.

"Yeah!" the boys cheered.

"And not only that," Ori said. "Zoë told me they didn't want to play babies with us ever again!"

The boys hugged good-bye, they were so happy. Then Dad and Jasper walked the rest of the way home. Jasper said he was so happy that he thought he might cry. He said, "What I need right now is a potholder."

They went quietly into the house in case Mom was still asleep. She was. She was stretched out on the sofa with the little blue notebook lying on the floor beside her. Jasper picked it up and showed it to Dad.

"This book explains why Mom is so tired," he whispered.

Dad took it and flipped through the pages. "Wow."

Jasper nodded.

"I feel bad," Dad said.

"Why?"

"Most of these things are things she does for us, Jasper. But what do we do for her?"

"A lot," Jasper said, spreading his arms wide. "We love her so so so so much!"

Chapter 14

The girls didn't bother Jasper and Ori and Leon and Paul C. again. Not that week, anyway. But on Monday after school, a Very Dangerous thing happened. When Ori and Jasper came out to meet Mom, Isabel was there with Mandy. "Look!" Ori said.

Jasper heard it before he saw it — a loud, buzzing sound.

"Be careful, Izzy," Mandy was saying. "Can't you see you're scaring everybody?"

The buzzing came from the remote-control car

that Isabel was zooming around the schoolyard.

Ori rushed over. "Can I try, Isabel? Can I?"

"Just a second, Ori," Isabel said, steering the car so it circled faster and faster around them. Then she handed the control to Ori and showed him how it worked.

Ori drove the car. It stopped and started like it was running out of gas.

"Like this," Isabel said, snatching the control back and sending the car buzzing off in a cloud of dust.

"Wow!" Ori said.

"Ori," Mom called. "We're leaving."

"Just a second! One more try!"

Isabel let him, and while Ori was driving, she asked, "Do you want to come to my house for a playdate, Ori?"

"Can we play with your car?" Ori asked.

"Sure! We can play anything you want. What's your phone number?"

Ori did the Very Dangerous thing then. He told Isabel his phone number. And she repeated it back until she memorized it.

"Ori!" Mom called.

"Bye, Ori!" Isabel called after him. "Bye! See you tomorrow, Ori! See you!"

"Stop shouting at him, Izzy," Mandy said. "Can't you see he's running away?"

Ori ran all the way to where Jasper and Mom were waiting for him at the corner of the schoolyard.

Jasper leaned close to Ori, his friend and neighbor and reading buddy and fellow knight. He leaned close enough to smell Ori. Ori smelled like celery. Then —

"Yuck!" Ori roared when he felt Jasper's wet tongue on his cheek. "Yuck!"

"Jasper!" Mom said. "I can't believe it! Did you just *lick* Ori?"

Ori wiped his cheek and yucked again.

"Why did you do that?" Mom asked Jasper. "Why?"

Before he could answer, Ori said, "I know why."

He smiled at Jasper, and Jasper smiled back.

"Can Jasper come to my house for a playdate?" Ori asked.

Don't miss Jasper John Dooley's other hilarious adventures!

Jasper John Dooley: Star of the Week
HCJ 978-1-55453-578-1
PB 978-1-77138-119-2

Jasper John Dooley: Left Behind
HCJ 978-1-55453-579-8

www.kidscanpress.com

KIDS CAN PRESS

Kids Can Press is a *CORUS*™ Entertainment company